I SURVIVED

THE DESTRUCTION OF POMPEII, AD 79

I SURVIVED

THE SINKING OF THE *TITANIC*, 1912

THE SHARK ATTACKS OF 1916

HURRICANE KATRINA, 2005

THE BOMBING OF PEARL HARBOR, 1941

THE SAN FRANCISCO EARTHQUAKE, 1906

THE ATTACKS OF SEPTEMBER 11, 2001

THE BATTLE OF GETTYSBURG, 1863

THE JAPANESE TSUNAMI, 2011

THE NAZI INVASION, 1944

THE DESTRUCTION OF POMPEII, AD 79

I SURVIVED

THE DESTRUCTION OF POMPEII, AD 79

by Lauren Tarshis

illustrated by Scott Dawson

Scholastic Inc.

For Barry Tarshis, my Tata

No part of this publication may be reproduced, stored in a retrieval system, or transmitted in any form or by any means, electronic, mechanical, photocopying, recording, or otherwise, without written permission of the publisher. For information regarding permission, write to: Scholastic Inc., Attention: Permissions Department, 557 Broadway, New York, NY 10012

ISBN 978-0-545-45939-6

17 16 15 14 13 12   16 17 18 19/0

Printed in the U.S.A.   40
First printing, September 2014
Designed by Yaffa Jaskoll
Series design by Tim Hall

CHAPTER 1

AUGUST 24, AD 79
1:00 P.M.
THE CITY OF POMPEII
THE ROMAN EMPIRE

Within hours, thousands of people would be dead.

The entire city of Pompeii would vanish under more than thirty feet of fiery ash and stone.

But first, it was a bright, sunny summer day. Shops bustled. Kids played ball in a grassy field. Gladiators readied for a bloody match.

Nobody yet knew that the mountain Vesuvius, which loomed over the city, was actually a deadly volcano. The mountain had been silent for centuries, a giant green triangle covered with farms and meadows and forests.

It was impossible to imagine what lurked under the ground — rivers of boiling magma, swirls of poisonous gases. Any moment, the mountain would erupt with devastating fury.

Eleven-year-old Marcus was with his father, Tata. They shouldn't have been anywhere near Pompeii. They were escaped slaves, running for their lives from evil men.

But then:

BOOM!

BOOM!

With two shattering explosions, Vesuvius erupted.

Thousands of pairs of eyes turned toward the mountain, staring in shock and terror. Black, billowing smoke and ash gushed out of the mountain's gaping mouth. Vesuvius roared like a furious beast, breathing smoke and flames into the sky. And then came an even bigger cloud, shooting out billions of hot, jagged rocks that rained down on Pompeii, filling fountains, crushing roofs, and pounding down on people as they tried to flee, screaming in panic.

"The gods are punishing us!"

"The world is ending!"

Marcus and Tata knew they had to escape. Any minute a flaming wave of ash and gases would rush down the mountain, burning everything in its path. But there were too many people in the streets, too many rocks falling from the sky. It was hard to breathe, almost impossible to see. And then there was the strange whooshing sound that came from above.

"Look out!" Tata shouted.

Marcus looked up just in time to see a massive flaming boulder falling from the sky, a chunk of fiery rock from deep inside the mountain.

It was heading right for them.

CHAPTER 2

AUGUST 23, AD 79
THE AFTERNOON BEFORE
MAIN STREET, POMPEII

Marcus walked along the dusty main street of
Pompeii, carrying a smelly sack stuffed with his
master's dirty laundry. It was early afternoon, and
the street was packed with people — shoppers
sifting through bins of pomegranates and melons,
weary slaves collecting water from the fountains,
beggars holding out their grimy hands.

A snake charmer dozed while his cobra peeked out of its basket, tasting the air with its flicking tongue.

"*Salve*," Marcus said, a friendly Latin hello for the deadly reptile. If only he had a basket to hide in right now. There were no good days for Marcus lately, but this day was sure to be more miserable than usual.

It was broiling hot and his ragged tunic was soaked in sweat. Even worse, his master, Festus Julius, was expecting important guests from Rome this evening, friends of the emperor. This meant even more backbreaking work than usual for Marcus and the other slaves. For days they'd been scrubbing the villa so that the mosaic floors shined like diamonds, so that every silver bowl and goblet gleamed.

The guests would arrive by chariot — men in flowing white togas, women in silk robes and with painted red lips, jewels flashing from every finger. Tonight there would be a great feast of roasted flamingo and wild boar, honey-baked mice stuffed with raisins and dates, and lobsters as big as cats. The guests would lounge on silken couches and gorge themselves until they threw up . . . and then, their stomachs empty, they would eat more.

Tomorrow, Festus would take them all to the gladiator fight at Pompeii's amphitheater. From front-row seats, they would cheer as the warriors tried to stab one another to death with swords, spears, and daggers.

People were coming from all over to see the spectacle, which featured Pompeii's champion fighter. He was a giant of a man, who had lost an eye in one of his early battles. The injury had earned him the fighting name of Cyclops, after the one-eyed monster from the old Greek tales. Like almost all gladiators, Cyclops was a slave who was forced to fight. But he was one of the lucky few — still alive after many battles.

Just thinking about these brutal tournaments horrified Marcus.

Suddenly his whole body was shaking.

But wait, it wasn't Marcus who was trembling. It was the earth beneath his feet!

Marcus dropped his sack and braced himself against a stone fountain. A huge marble statue of the warrior Achilles looked down on him.

Marcus wished he felt as brave as Achilles!

But these tremors spooked him. For weeks they'd been shaking the city, putting cracks in the walls of Festus's villa, sending his spoiled dogs into fits of howling.

Usually the quakes were quick, ending in just a few seconds. Most people seemed to barely notice them.

But this quake was more powerful than most.

The ground shuddered and shook, harder and harder.

Up and down the street, the sound of shattering glass and splintering wood and crumbling stone pounded Marcus's ears.

Crash!
Crack!
Bang!

Vendors cursed as their baskets of fruit and vegetables toppled. A bamboo birdcage fell and burst open, scattering a flock of tiny white birds into the dusty air. Barrels rolled wildly through the streets, gushing wine as red as blood.

Marcus held tight to the fountain as the water inside it sloshed, splashing over the rim and soaking his tunic.

And then he heard it, a creaking just over his head. Marcus looked up just as the massive marble statue of Achilles came crashing down on top of him.

CHAPTER 3

Marcus dove to the ground, his chin smacking the hard stone. He braced himself for the crushing blow of thousands of pounds of marble hitting him. He heard a terrible *crash*!

But he felt nothing.

He peeled open his eyes and peered around.

To his amazement, the broken statue was just behind him. It must have sailed right over him. Marcus whispered a thank-you to the gods.

Poor Achilles had lost his head, which was now rolling slowly in the street.

Marcus could practically hear the warrior's deathly cries.

But Marcus himself was in one piece, and the earth had stopped shaking.

Marcus pulled himself up. He put his hand to his chin, and it came away streaked with blood. Otherwise he was unhurt.

A humpbacked street vendor came up to him. "Don't even think about stealing those apples," he barked, reaching down and snatching two apples that had escaped from his baskets.

"I wouldn't," Marcus said, spotting a third hidden behind the fountain. He should give it to the man, he knew. But just the thought of the juicy apple made his stomach flip with joy. Festus fed his slaves nothing but watery gruel and old cheese. The fruit seller didn't spot it, and Marcus said nothing.

"That giant beast must be restless," said the man, spitting on one of the apples and rubbing it against his rough tunic.

"Giant?" Marcus asked.

"Everyone knows that's why the earth is shaking," the man replied, looking at Marcus as though he must be stupid not to know this. "There's a great beast living under the mountain. Every few years it wakes up and the city shakes. Then it goes to sleep again."

Marcus thought of his father — Tata. Talk of monsters and magic always made Tata shake his head. Tata said it was only natural that people would make up stories or blame the gods for what they couldn't understand — wild storms and killing fevers, dead crops and mad dogs. But science always held the answer, Tata believed, if you looked hard enough.

Marcus didn't say this now. It wasn't right for a slave to correct the opinion of a free man, even if the man was just a poor fruit seller.

What amazed Marcus was that people in Pompeii just accepted these tremors, shrugging them off as they would a rainstorm. Even now, shoppers were already back to haggling for bargains.

The fruit seller turned away and Marcus

grabbed the hidden apple, slipping it into his pocket. He picked up the heavy laundry sack and threw it onto his back with a sigh. Festus wouldn't care if a monster really had come stomping through Pompeii. Marcus had better get back to his master's villa soon, or he'd be greeted with a beating.

He was turning to leave when he noticed an old woman sitting in the street, dazed. The shaking must have knocked her down. Passersby stepped around her as if she were a heap of trash. Marcus ignored the woman; there were beggars everywhere, after all.

But she looked so miserable.

With a sigh, he once again dropped the laundry sack. He went to the woman, crouching down next to her. She was a beggar, it seemed, her tunic stained and tattered, her bare feet crusted with sores.

She scowled at him. "Scat, thief!"

"I wasn't going to steal anything," Marcus said. He should have ignored the hag like everyone else did.

But then the woman's face softened. She studied Marcus with her catlike green eyes. She was very old, with sagging cheeks and deep wrinkles. But Marcus could imagine that a long time ago she might have been pretty.

"What do you want, then?" she asked.

Almost without thinking, he reached into his pocket and took out the apple. "Here," he said. She looked hungrier than he was.

The woman took the apple in one of her gnarled hands. "Help me up, please."

Marcus held her arms as she got to her feet, and stood with her as she steadied herself. And then she suddenly grabbed his hand, gripping it with surprising strength.

"Be careful, kind boy," she whispered. "I have seen the signs. Terrible doom is coming for the people of Pompeii."

She leaned so close that he smelled the strange spices on her breath.

"When hope is lost, *follow the hand of Mercury*." She stepped back. "Do you understand?"

Marcus had no idea what she meant. All over Pompeii there were statues of the powerful messenger god, with his winged sandals and helmet. But what did that matter to him?

"I understand," he lied. Now he just wanted to get away from her.

"The end is coming," she said, finally letting go of his hand. "This world will burn!"

CHAPTER 4

Marcus had barely blinked and the woman was gone, swallowed by the crowd.

He felt a stab of fear as he thought of what she had said.

Was she a witch who could predict the future? A priestess who could hear the whispers of the gods?

Marcus thought again of his father. Tata would know what was happening here.

A wave of sadness crashed over him. If only Tata were with him now!

He could picture his father so clearly — his gentle blue eyes glinting through a mop of golden hair.

Tata was born in Germania, a kingdom just beyond the northern boundaries of this vast Roman Empire. When Tata was just ten years old, Roman soldiers had invaded his village. Marcus's father was soon captured, sold to slave traders, and marched hundreds of miles in chains to the empire's capital city of Rome.

But Tata was lucky. He was bought by a kind man, a writer and scientist named Linus Selius. He taught Tata to read and write in Latin, the language of the empire. He took Tata on research trips to faraway lands, teaching him all he knew about the natural world. Soon, Tata was helping Linus research his books and coming up with theories of his own.

The years passed. Tata married Marcus's mother, who died when Marcus was just a baby. Marcus grew up helping Tata in Linus's library, one of the finest in Rome.

Tata was always trying to get Marcus interested in studying nature, reading him his latest theories and dragging him on long walks through the hills above Rome.

But it was the ancient Greek stories written centuries before that Marcus loved most, especially the tales of the great heroes like Odysseus and Hercules.

How Marcus had loved his happy life with Tata!

But then, two months ago, Linus Selius had died in a fever that swept through Rome. In a blink, Marcus's entire world crumbled. Marcus and Tata became the property of Linus's nephew, the brutal Festus Julius. Linus himself had always despised Festus, and the nephew wasted no time destroying his uncle's happy home. Within two days, Tata was sold. Marcus was loaded onto a donkey cart and brought here to Pompeii, a two-day trip from Rome. He was now one of ten slaves working endless days in Festus's enormous villa, one of the grandest homes in Pompeii.

Where was Tata? He could be anywhere in the vast Roman Empire by now, from the rocky cliffs of Britannia to the deserts of Africa.

His thoughts carried Marcus far away, until a blaring trumpet yanked him back.

"It's the gladiator parade!" an old man cried out with excitement. "It's the fighters who will appear tomorrow!"

People jammed the sidewalks, so Marcus could not get through. Now he had no choice but to put down the laundry sack and wait.

Two men on white horses led the parade, their riders waving bright flags. A band of horn players followed, and then acrobats and jugglers, and finally, a stout man with a leering smile. He was the *lanista* — the owner of these gladiators.

The lanista waved at the crowd, proud as an emperor. Owning gladiators was a dirty business; no respectable person would do it. But the lanista had grown rich on the blood of his gladiators, and he held his head high.

And then there was Cyclops, led by two young women in bright robes who were throwing rose petals.

"There he is!" a woman in the crowd shrieked, pointing at the muscled brute.

The champion wore a gleaming bronze helmet. His massive shield matched the armor strapped to his bulging legs and arms. A leather patch hid his blind eye. Scars covered his face. Marcus had heard terrifying stories about this man — that he had jaws like a tiger's, that his battle cry was like a panther's scream, that he could snap a man's neck with one hand.

The crowd cheered and hooted as Cyclops passed.

But people stood silently as the next four men walked by. These were the wretched souls who would be thrown into the arena with Cyclops tomorrow. None of them had a chance against Cyclops. By tomorrow afternoon, they'd all be dead.

Marcus couldn't bear to watch them. But then he caught sight of the last man in line.

Marcus froze, staring.

The man was tall, with golden hair streaming out of his bronze helmet. He walked slowly, with dignity. A guard followed him, jabbing him in the back with a spear to move him along.

The man turned his head, and the sun lit up his proud face and glinting blue eyes.

Could it be?

The pounding in Marcus's heart told the answer.

And suddenly Marcus was running wildly into the street.

"Tata!" Marcus screamed.

CHAPTER 5

Tata froze and looked up, searching the crowd frantically with his eyes.

The guard screamed at him, "Move! Move now!"

At last Tata spotted Marcus. He dropped his shield and ran toward him. Seconds later, Marcus was in Tata's arms.

"It's not possible!" Tata whispered, hugging him so tightly that Marcus could hardly breathe. "How did you get here?"

"Festus brought me here after you were sold,"

Marcus said, barely able to choke out the words. "But Tata! How . . . why . . ."

Not even in Marcus's nightmares could he have imagined anything worse than this: Festus had sold Tata to the gladiators.

Marcus buried his face in Tata's chest, breathing in his familiar smell. Every day — every hour — Marcus had wished for this moment. And for a few seconds he let himself believe that they were really back together, that his prayers had been answered.

But, of course, the opposite was true.

Two guards grabbed Tata's arms, tearing him away from Marcus.

And then the lanista appeared.

"What's this!" he spat. "How dare you stop my parade!"

The musicians were silent, the jugglers and acrobats still. All eyes were on Tata and Marcus.

"Have mercy!" Tata said, struggling in the guards' grip. "This is my son!"

The lanista stared at Marcus, his cold, fishy eyes looking him up and down.

"Maybe you'd like to join your father in the arena?" he sneered.

Then the lanista looked to the crowd. "What do you think?" he bellowed. "A father and son against Cyclops!"

A few people shouted.

"Bring him!"

"Yes!"

"What a show it will be!"

"Or maybe you should fight each other?" the lanista said, rubbing his hands together.

"Run from here, Marcus!" his father cried. "Go!"

But instead, Marcus grabbed the lanista's arm. "I beg you! Please let my father go!"

The man ripped his arm away and snatched a spear from one of the guards. He pointed the blade at Marcus's eye. "Ever wondered how Cyclops lost his eye?" he taunted, lunging at Marcus.

"No!" Tata shouted.

Marcus staggered back. He lost his balance and fell, smacking his head on the stone curb. His head exploded in pain. He struggled to sit up, and through the blur he could see Tata being dragged away, the guards jabbing him with spears. The lanista's wicked cackle rose up over the merry music.

As Tata disappeared, all of the strength drained from Marcus's body. These past two months, he'd always had the hope that he and Tata would be together again. And that speck of hope — a tiny glowing ember — had been everything to him.

But now . . .

Marcus lay back in the gutter, closing his eyes.

How would he go on?

In his mind he pictured Festus's face, heard his barking orders. He imagined the slaves who'd been working in the villa for years. Their bodies were crooked and scarred, their eyes dead like statues'.

And then Marcus thought of the heroes from his favorite stories. They had desperate moments, too: Odysseus, who was lost at sea for ten years on his way home from Troy. Hercules, pinned down by a bloodthirsty lion.

Those courageous men knew terror and hopelessness, as Marcus did now.

But their stories hadn't ended with fear and defeat.

Marcus's eyes snapped open. He sat up and struggled to his feet.

He understood.

He would try to save Tata, even if it killed him.

CHAPTER 6

Marcus went to the fountain and splashed cool water on his face.

He didn't have much time. Soon the parade would reach the gladiator barracks, and Tata would be locked away. The barracks was like a prison, with high stone walls and a towering iron gate. Marcus had heard that the fighters were locked in dark cells, their arms and legs shackled, until it was time to fight.

Once Tata was in the barracks, it would be too late.

Somehow, Marcus had to steal Tata away from the parade.

But how?

He searched his mind for ideas. Again, he thought of Odysseus.

Odysseus wasn't the strongest man. But he was cunning. There had come a low point in the Trojan War when the Greek armies had Troy surrounded, but they could not break through the massive wall that encircled the city. Thousands of Trojan archers guarded the wall, ready to fire down on anyone who came close. Some Greek generals were ready to give up on invading the city of Troy.

Not Odysseus.

He came up with the ingenious idea of building a giant wooden horse with a hollow belly. He and his best Greek soldiers hid inside the horse. They made the Trojans believe the wooden animal was an offering from the gods, and tricked them into bringing it inside their walls.

And then — *attack!*

In the dead of night, Odysseus and the hidden soldiers snuck out of the horse and opened the gates. The Greek soldiers smashed the Trojan army and conquered the city.

Marcus searched around. All he saw was the laundry bag, lying where he had dropped it.

But wait . . .

The idea flashed into Marcus's mind, and before he could talk himself out of it, he had ripped the sack open and was rummaging through Festus's clothes.

He grabbed a toga, a robe woven from the finest wool and edged with purple ribbon. Marcus couldn't build himself a wooden horse. But he could hide in Festus's toga, disguise himself as an important Roman citizen.

Marcus threw it around himself, covering his old tunic. The toga stank like rotten food, old wine, and Festus's sweat. Marcus fought back his nausea as he wrapped the endless stretch of fabric around his body, finally draping the loose end over his shoulder.

He straightened his shoulders. The toga dragged on the ground a bit, but it would do. Marcus spat into his hands and flattened his hair to his forehead, the style of a rich son of Rome.

Now he just needed a weapon, something to scare the guards so he and Tata could escape.

Once again, the answer was right in front of him, on the sidewalk: the snake charmer.

Somehow, the old man was still dozing with the basket at his feet.

Marcus crept up, kneeled, and snatched the basket.

The old man was awake in a flash, hollering after him. "Stop him! Stop that thief!"

Marcus darted through the crowd, one hand firmly on the lid of the basket. He was terrified that the lid would fly off, that the cobra would spring out and sink its fangs into Marcus's neck. He could feel the snake hissing ferociously, banging its body against the sides of the flimsy basket.

Marcus's heart pounded, his legs wobbled, his mind swirled with fear. But somehow he kept himself moving until he caught up with the parade.

The music had stopped and the lanista was unlocking the gates of the gladiator barracks.

Marcus was almost out of time.

And he would have just one chance.

CHAPTER 7

Marcus stepped slowly, clutching the basket. At first he didn't notice how people moved aside for him, how slaves bowed their heads. And then he understood: His disguise was working! Nobody guessed he was just a slave.

None of the guards tried to stop him as he approached the front of the parade. Marcus saw the lanista, his chest puffed out. And there was Tata. The big guard was jabbing him in the back with a spear, laughing at Tata's pain.

Marcus's blood boiled as he walked toward the lanista.

Closer . . .

Closer . . .

Closer . . .

When he was just a few feet away, the lanista looked at him. Their eyes met, and Marcus saw the flash of recognition in the man's eyes.

"Stop him!" the lanista bellowed, pointing to Marcus.

But it was too late. Marcus tore the lid off the basket. He lunged forward. And with all the strength he could gather, he thrust the open basket toward the lanista, propelling the snake into the air.

The cobra soared, a twisting, hissing arrow. The snake struck the lanista in the chest and then landed on the ground, coiling itself tightly.

The lanista's womanly scream rose up over the crowd.

And everything went still and silent.

People stared, hypnotized by the sight of the cobra.

The creature lifted its head, rising, rising, rising, until it was as tall as a child. It flared its great hood and then opened its mouth to expose its silky pink mouth and killer fangs.

Hisssssssssssssssssssssssssssssssssss!

And then, as if Marcus himself had pulled a lever, the earth started to rumble, just as it had earlier. Stones crumbled and fell from the wall surrounding the barracks. A roar echoed from deep under the ground.

"It's a curse from the gods!" someone shouted.

The crowd erupted in panic.

The lanista turned and ran, and his guards followed.

Gladiators bolted. The snake slithered away.

The horses screeched and reared up, tossing their riders to the ground.

Marcus ran to Tata, who stared at him in confusion.

"Tata!" Marcus said, tossing off his toga. "It's me!"

Amazement lit up Tata's eyes, but there was not a second to spare.

Tata grabbed Marcus's hand as though he would never let it go.

"This way!" Tata said, pulling Marcus to one of the riderless horses. It was a ragged white mare that looked a hundred years old. One of her ears looked as if it had been chewed off. Tata grabbed the reins and soothed the horse while Marcus climbed on. Tata climbed on in front of Marcus. "Hold on tight," he said, snapping the reins.

Marcus doubted the old horse could even run. But she shot forward and was soon speeding them down the street.

Marcus clung to Tata, his heart pounding in terror. He expected spears to fly after them, a dagger to stab him in the middle of his back. But the horse ran faster and faster; it seemed she was as eager to escape her life in Pompeii as they were.

They moved so fast that Marcus felt as though they were flying. Closing his eyes, he imagined that this old white mare was the winged horse Pegasus, and that they were soaring through the clouds.

When he opened his eyes, he was shocked to see they had passed through the city gates.

Tata raised his fist to the heavens and let out a Latin cheer.

"Ecce!"

They had made it.

CHAPTER 8

THAT AFTERNOON
THE ROAD TO VESUVIUS

They headed for the mountain Vesuvius, a massive triangle of green that loomed up to the east of Pompeii. As they left the city behind, Tata ripped the armor from his shoulders and legs, and threw the pieces into a ditch. He left his helmet in a field of wheat, a trade for the old tunic he snatched from the farmer's drying line.

They rode for hours, crossing orchards and olive groves, pastures and fields.

Night was coming, and Tata decided they should stop in a patch of woods halfway up the mountain.

They got off the mare and stretched their aching legs.

Marcus reached into his pocket and pulled out a handful of grapes he'd snatched from a vineyard they'd passed through.

"Hungry, Peg?" Marcus said to the mare.

"Peg?" Tata asked, arching one of his bushy brows.

"Short for Pegasus," Marcus said.

Tata smiled, stroking the mare's nose.

Marcus fed the grapes to Peg one by one, until they were all gone.

Peg smacked her lips and rubbed Marcus's cheek with her nose.

"We have a friend for life, it seems," Tata said.

Peg nickered as though she agreed, and Marcus and Tata laughed.

It was that moment, as their laughter filled the air, that it really hit Marcus: This was not a dream, not a wish, not a desperate prayer to the gods.

He and Tata were together! A jolt of happiness practically lifted him off the ground. And Tata seemed to feel it, too. They looked at each other and smiled.

But then a shadow passed over Marcus's heart. Because as happy as he felt at this moment, he knew they were in terrible danger.

"They'll come after us," Marcus whispered.

The slave hunters. Festus would hire the best, most cunning men, experts in tracking their prey.

"They won't look for us up here," Tata promised. "The hunters will be searching Pompeii. It will be days before they come to the mountain. And by then we'll be gone. We'll head back to Rome, Marcus. I have no doubt that Linus's friends will help us. Somehow I need to continue Linus's work."

It amazed Marcus that Tata could be so certain, so filled with hope. He draped an arm around

Marcus's shoulders and looked up into the sky, admiring the bright moon and the swirl of stars.

But what Marcus saw in the bright moonlight was the angry bruise on Tata's cheek, the purple scar zigzagging along his chin. How Tata must have suffered these past two months!

Marcus had already told Tata about his time with Festus. The words had poured out of him during their ride up the mountain, until at last he had told Tata about every last moment of his time with his brutal master.

But Tata hadn't said a thing about being with the gladiators.

And now Marcus wanted to know.

"Will you tell me what happened to you, Tata?" Marcus said.

Pain flashed through Tata's eyes and he looked away from Marcus.

"That is the past now," he said.

And from his tone, Marcus knew that he must not ask again.

But he couldn't help thinking about what his father must have been through. And it made his blood boil.

"I hate that lanista!" Marcus burst out. "And I hate Festus! I hate all of them for what they did to you, Tata! We need to get even!"

Yes, Marcus thought, they'd get revenge! They'd set fire to Festus's villa! Find the lanista and . . .

But Tata whipped around, gripping Marcus's shoulders.

"No, Marcus," he snapped. "Never speak like

that. You must never let hatred take over! Then you are no better than Festus! And hatred like that will destroy you."

Marcus blinked, stung by Tata's sharp tone.

"I'm sorry, Tata," Marcus said.

Tata's face softened. "There is goodness in the world, Marcus, and kindness. You cannot forget that."

Goodness? Kindness?

Marcus had seen none of that lately.

If there was one thing Marcus had learned these past two months, it was this: The world was a dark, evil place. Only the most ruthless would survive.

But Marcus said none of that to Tata, who would not approve of such dark thoughts.

And they were both so tired. They led Peg into a small grove of trees and tied her up for the night.

Tata stretched out on a grassy patch.

"Tomorrow our new life begins," he whispered, and within seconds he was fast asleep.

Marcus lay down next to Tata, but he couldn't get comfortable. His muscles ached from the long ride. But it was the strange noises that kept snapping him awake — distant rumbles, low hisses. Was he dreaming? Once, he drifted to sleep, but was awakened when the earth seemed to be shaking. He sat up, wondering if Tata felt it, too.

But Tata was sound asleep.

Was Marcus imagining things? Maybe what he was hearing were just the rumbles of his own angry heart.

But Peg seemed restless, too, stamping her feet, snorting.

Finally Marcus got up and stood with her, stroking her patchy fur, resting his cheek against her warm head. He looked down at Pompeii, dimly lit by oil lamps and torches. He made out the shapes of the houses crowded together along the city walls, the boats moored in the harbor.

Marcus hugged Peg.

"It's okay," he told her. "We're with Tata now. We're safe up here."

He knew that was true, that the slave hunters were far away, that Festus was too busy with his important guests to be thinking too much about his escaped slave.

Still, Marcus couldn't shake the feeling that there was something lurking up here on the mountain, something even more dangerous than the slave hunters.

But what could it be?

CHAPTER 9

It was close to dawn when Marcus finally fell asleep.

And right away, he tumbled into a dream.

He was on a quest with Hercules to kill the monstrous Hydra, an enormous serpent with nine heads. Just one puff of her poisonous breath could kill.

Marcus waded silently through the dark and misty swamp, pushing aside sharp stalks of grass. And then, just ahead, there she was: the hideous serpent. Marcus stopped, frozen, as the beast rose

up from the swamp. One by one, her nine horrific heads emerged from the mist, staring at him with glowing yellow eyes, leering with dripping, glistening fangs.

And then —

Huff.

A burning, rotten stench rushed into Marcus's lungs.

The poisonous Hydra breath!

Marcus gagged and coughed.

47

His throat burned. His chest felt as if it would explode!

"Marcus! Marcus!" a voice called.

Hercules?

"Marcus!"

Marcus's eyes popped open, and the nightmare fell away. Tata was kneeling next to him, calling his name, shaking him awake.

It was all a dream!

Relief poured over him as he realized he wasn't in a swamp with the Hydra. He was on the mountain Vesuvius, with Tata.

But wait . . . something was terribly wrong.

The air was still poisonous! The Hydra was still puffing gusts of her burning breath into Marcus's lungs.

But there was no Hydra.

That burning, poisonous smell was *here*.

"Marcus," Tata choked. "Get up! The air has gone bad!"

Tata helped pull Marcus to his feet and they staggered together toward Peg.

Marcus's head pounded. Tears poured from his stinging eyes. His lungs were on fire and he gasped for breath. He felt dizzy. They couldn't last much longer in this air!

Peg was rearing in panic, white foam spewing from her mouth.

Tata fumbled with her rope, finally untying it.

They all stumbled out of the grove of trees, where the air was miraculously clear.

Tata and Marcus collapsed to the ground, gulping the fresh air into their lungs.

"Tata," Marcus rasped. "What was that?"

"Sulfur gas," Tata replied, his voice ragged from coughing. "There's no doubt. I smelled it once before, when Linus and I were visiting a gold mine in Africa. We were deep underground. Sulfur gas can be deadly. It can kill in minutes. We barely made it to the surface in time."

Tata looked back into the grove of trees. "It's highly unusual to find sulfur gas above the ground," he said.

He stood and climbed onto a boulder that

jutted out from the grassy slope, looking all around. Marcus saw a hint of worry in his father's eyes. But mainly what he saw was curiosity, a hunger to learn and understand. It was the same look Tata used to get in Linus Selius's library when he was chasing down a new theory. Suddenly, Tata was not a slave on the run. He was a scientist, searching for answers.

And the truth was that after spending a lifetime working with Linus, Tata probably knew more about science and nature than most people in the empire. In recent years, Linus would ask Tata to join him when important guests came, eager for his friends to hear Tata's ideas.

Tata hopped down from the boulder.

He held out his hand to Marcus, pulling him to his feet.

"Let's keep heading up the mountain," he said, handing Marcus Peg's reins. "We'll discover more as we get closer to the top."

Tata set out, climbing the rocky path.

Marcus took a deep breath, and gave Peg's reins a tug.

But the mare didn't budge.

She looked at Marcus with her wise brown eyes. Her expression was so thoughtful. Marcus would not have been shocked if she had opened her mouth and started to speak to him.

"What is it?" Marcus said.

The mare looked up the mountain.

She stamped her foot.

"You don't want to go up there, do you?"

Snort.

"Me neither," Marcus said.

Tata's voice shouted out. "Marcus!"

Marcus and Peg eyed each other.

"We can't let Tata head up there by himself," Marcus said.

Peg made a noise that sounded like a sigh, and she stepped forward.

Together they followed Tata toward the top of Vesuvius.

CHAPTER 10

AUGUST 24

7:00 A.M.

THE MOUNTAIN VESUVIUS

They took the twisting path that wound up the mountain.

The sun was barely up, but already it roasted their backs.

Tata kept stopping to look around. He seemed to be taking the mountain apart with his eyes, inch by inch. He kept crouching down, scooping up handfuls of soil, rubbing it between his fingers. He ripped up pieces of grass, sniffing them, and even touching them to his tongue.

"Do you notice the quiet?" he asked at one point. "There are no birds or insects anywhere."

Tata was right.

Normally at this time of morning, the air would be alive with chirping and singing and chattering. But Marcus had not seen one creature since they came up on the mountain, not a deer, a squirrel, nor even a fly. No people, either. There were pastures on this side of Vesuvius, and they'd passed two shepherd shacks. But they hadn't seen a soul.

"Where did they all go?" Marcus asked, trying to keep his voice from shaking.

"It might be that there's not enough water," Tata said. "It could be the heat drove them off."

They'd already discovered that the streams higher up on the mountain were mysteriously dried up. They'd managed to find just one that still ran. And the trickle of water tasted so foul they could barely choke it down. Peg wouldn't go near it, even though she'd barely had a drink since before they'd slept last night. Maybe that was why she was walking so slowly, why she kept stopping and stamping her feet.

But now, as they passed through a cluster of pine trees, Peg stopped short. Tata pulled at her rope, but she refused to move. Marcus gave her a pat.

"Come on, Peg," he said.

The mare refused to budge.

She looked at Marcus with wide, fearful eyes.

Neigh!

Was she trying to warn them about something?

Marcus found the answer when he peered through the trees, into a meadow. The first thing he noticed was the grass was brown, as though it had been burned.

Then he saw the sheep — at least twenty of them — all splayed out on their sides or backs.

Marcus knew right away that they were all dead.

"Good Jupiter," Tata whispered in shock, stepping slowly into the field.

Once again, Marcus had to force himself to follow his father.

Tata crouched down next to one of the sheep.

"There's not a mark on her," Tata said, laying a gentle hand over the poor creature's head.

It was true — there was not a speck of blood, no bite marks, no wounds at all.

But her tongue bulged out of her mouth and her eyes were wide in agony.

All the sheep looked the same.

What could have killed them?

Tata said a prayer in his old Germanic language and then stood up.

"I've seen enough," he said. "We must leave here. Now."

But as they turned, there was a low rumbling from deep inside the earth. It quickly rose to a roar as the ground started to shake. Marcus half expected a great beast to burst through the soil, for a giant clawed hand to grab him around the throat.

What he saw next was almost more horrifying.

As the ground boiled, the field suddenly ripped apart right in front of them. The gaping crack looked like an evil smiling mouth, ready to devour them. Great chunks of earth and dead sheep tumbled into the blackness. Marcus and Tata staggered back.

And then —

Boom!

An explosion shattered the air. Fire leaped out of the crack, a massive flaming tongue that seemed to lick the sky and then disappear.

The force of the blast knocked them over, and sent Marcus tumbling down the steep slope.

He rolled and twisted, his neck cracking, his arms tangling, his face scraping the rocky dirt as he slid down the hill.

He crashed into a tree, which knocked every bit of air out of his lungs.

Finally the ground stopped shaking. The fire was gone. But now ash rained down on them, a silent blizzard of hot flakes.

Marcus sat there, numb with terror, dizzy from his fall.

Tata came hurtling down the hill with Peg.

"Are you hurt?" he gasped, dropping to his knees next to Marcus.

Marcus shook his head dumbly, slowly rising to his feet.

Moments later, they were speeding down the mountain on Peg.

The mare ran like she had the day before, her hooves barely touching the ground.

Finally, Tata spoke.

"A terrible fire is burning under the mountain," he warned. "I believe the entire mountain will explode."

Marcus was too stunned to speak, or even think.

All he could hear was a ragged voice whispering in his mind.

The beggar woman's voice.

"This world will burn."

CHAPTER 11

Tata was silent for most of the ride down, hunkered deep inside his thoughts. Marcus could sense that he was trying to assemble a huge puzzle in his mind, to make sense out of all they had seen.

As they came to the bottom of the mountain, Tata had his theory, and he explained it all to Marcus in terrifying detail.

"Some mountains are not just solid rock," Tata began. "They are filled with gases and fire and melted rock. Virgil wrote about such a mountain in Greece, called Etna."

Virgil was one of Rome's most famous writers.

"Virgil told of a terrible eruption, maybe a hundred years ago," Tata continued. "He said that fire and ash shot from the mountain into the sky, that day turned to night, and a burning cloud swept down the mountain, destroying everything in its path."

Tata turned to look at Marcus.

"I never imagined it could be true," Tata said. "I thought it was just an exciting tale. But now we've seen for ourselves."

Yes, they had, though Marcus still couldn't quite believe it had all happened. The earth tremors. Killer clouds. Foul water. Dead sheep. Flames shooting out of the ground. And that terrifying explosion. It was stranger than any tale Marcus had ever read.

"It all makes sense," Tata said. "What is happening now on Vesuvius tells me that the worst is yet to come, that the entire mountain is about to explode."

Marcus shivered, though the heat was searing.

"Will Pompeii be destroyed?" he said.

Tata was silent for a moment.

"I have no doubt," Tata said finally.

Marcus held Tata tighter.

"I met an old woman yesterday, a beggar," he said, remembering the woman's shining green eyes and gnarled hands. "She said the strangest things to me — that Pompeii was doomed, that the city would burn. I thought she was a madwoman. But what she said was right! She could read the future!"

"I don't believe in prophets and witches," Tata said. "But nature sends out warnings. Why do you think all of the animals have fled? They felt the tremors, scented the sulfur, tasted the water. Their instincts told them to flee. Linus would say that the old woman is keenly sensitive — or that she has the mind of a great scientist."

It was hard to imagine that poor old hag discussing science with Tata and Linus. But what Tata said made sense.

"Where will we go?" Marcus asked.

Tata didn't answer right away.

Then he slowed Peg to a stop and turned in the saddle to face Marcus.

"We need to warn the people of Pompeii," he said. "They have no idea what is about to happen. If we don't warn them, they could all be killed."

It took Marcus a moment for Tata's words to sink in.

Was he really saying they should go to the very city about to be destroyed? A city where slave hunters were prowling through every alley with their spears and chains?

Marcus didn't want to go anywhere near that wretched city! He and Tata needed to save themselves, to get as far away as they could. Now!

"I don't understand," Marcus said.

Tata touched Marcus's hand. "But you do. There are more than ten thousand people living in Pompeii. It's our duty to warn them of what is about to happen."

Marcus tried to look away from Tata, but their eyes were locked together.

And Marcus recognized something in Tata's gaze.

It was the same determined look that Marcus had always imagined on the faces of his heroes as they prepared for their battles.

Hadn't Odysseus and Hercules risked their lives over and over? Hadn't they plunged into danger without thinking about whether they'd come out alive?

Marcus had read so many stories of heroic warriors. But it was only now, looking at his father, that he finally understood what it meant to have honor, to be a hero.

Marcus reached deep inside himself, trying to summon some courage of his own.

To his surprise, he found more than he expected.

He sat taller. "Yes, I understand, Tata."

Marcus saw the flash of pride on Tata's face before he turned back around. He gave Peg a pat.

And off they galloped, on their tattered mare, toward the doomed city of Pompeii.

CHAPTER 12

The sun was high in the sky as they approached the city.

They tied Peg to a tree in an olive grove, about a half mile from Pompeii's eastern gates.

Marcus hugged Peg. "I'll be back."

The mare nosed him in the chest, looking him in the eye.

The ground rumbled again — the tremors were definitely getting stronger.

Marcus looked back nervously at the mountain and loosened Peg's rope.

"If we're not back, you need to break free from here and get out on your own."

Peg eyed him.

"You understand me?" he said. "Don't wait for us."

The mare snorted.

Marcus hoped that meant yes.

He hugged her one last time, and Tata rubbed her nose before they headed for the city gates.

Tata's plan was to speak to Pompeii's magistrates — the men elected to lead the city. They would know the best way to warn the people of Pompeii.

Marcus and Tata wove through the crowded streets, keeping their eyes out for men who might help — and those who might be hunting for them.

It didn't take long to reach the Forum — an open square surrounded by five buildings and the city's main temple, dedicated to Jupiter. Statues of emperors and generals seemed to glare at Marcus as he followed Tata to the magistrates' building. Marcus's heart pounded as they approached the entrance, where three steely-looking guards stood watch.

"Stop, slave," a guard ordered.

Tata held his head up.

"Sir, I have an urgent message for the city's leaders. The city is in danger. We must warn the people of Pompeii."

The man barely glanced at Tata from beneath his helmet.

"Be gone," the guard ordered, shooing him as though he were a stray dog.

"Sir," Tata said. "It's the mountain. There will soon be a terrible explosion. We —"

The guard raised his spear menacingly.

"Go from here! Nobody in there wants to talk to a filthy slave!"

Suddenly Marcus couldn't help but see what the guard saw when he looked at Tata. With his tattered tunic and body stained with bruises, Tata looked little better than the beggar woman.

The other guards stepped up, their spears glinting in the sun.

This was hopeless, Marcus realized.

"You are making a mistake," Tata warned, taking Marcus's arm and hurrying him away.

They walked out of the Forum and headed toward the main street.

"We'll have to tell people ourselves," Tata said. "We'll go to the shops and restaurants. Hopefully some people will listen."

Marcus hoped Tata couldn't read his thoughts: They were wasting their time. Nobody would take the word of a slave.

They stood on the sidewalk, waiting to cross the crowded street.

Two laughing little boys ran behind their mother. One held a wooden sword.

"I'm Cyclops!" the boy sang.

The gladiator match! That's where everyone was heading!

Marcus watched the boys, but then his eyes drifted up to Vesuvius.

What he saw stopped his heart: a wisp of smoke, rising out of the peak.

The mountain seemed to be coming alive.

"Tata . . ." Marcus pointed up at the smoking mountain.

Tata stared in horror — and fascination.

They both stood there, their eyes glued to the mountain. Which is why they didn't see the golden chariot that had stopped suddenly right in front of them — or the pair of cold, pale eyes that glared at them.

By the time Marcus saw Festus and his guards rushing toward them, it was too late. Penned in by the crowds, he and Tata were trapped.

And seconds later Marcus was staring at the glinting tip of a spear.

"Idiots," Festus hissed. "You actually believed you could escape?"

Tata shook his arm from the guard's grip and stepped toward Festus.

"Sir, please, a disaster is coming. The mountain is about to explode. People must leave the city right away."

Festus laughed cruelly. "You think you can save yourself by telling tales?"

The guard grabbed Tata roughly, and once again Tata shook himself free. He seemed to be gaining strength from the crowd, from the fear and panic in the eyes of the people all around them.

"You've felt the earth tremors. And now look

at the mountain. You can see for yourself, the smoke! Any moment it's going to explode."

Festus didn't even look at the mountain. He put his face close to Tata's, screaming, "You dare try to outsmart me? You think I'm a fool?"

"Think of your uncle, sir, of Linus," Tata said, struggling as the guard gripped him again. "He would agree with me. I'm certain."

Festus's fat cheeks turned bright red.

"My uncle was a weak-minded idiot," Festus said, spitting out the words. "He cared more for a slave than me, a man who shared his own blood!"

And suddenly it was all clear to Marcus — why Festus had sold Tata so quickly.

Few people in Rome were as admired as Linus Selius. And yet he had never been impressed by Festus's chariots and villas and fine stallions. Linus knew the truth about his nephew, that he made his money by cheating people.

Tata had the one thing that Festus's fortune couldn't buy: his uncle's respect.

And Festus hated Tata for it. He hated him so much that he would make Tata suffer the worst fate imaginable: death in the arena.

"Take this slave to the lanista!" Festus ordered. "He will be just in time for his match against Cyclops."

As the guards dragged his father away, Marcus's blood boiled in his veins. His heart smoldered with hatred.

He stepped close to Festus, looking him squarely in his fishlike eyes.

"You are evil."

"Marcus!" Tata gasped.

Marcus couldn't miss the flicker of shock on Festus's face.

But, of course, Festus had the last word.

"Take the boy to the lanista, too. Tell him it's a gift from me. It will be quite a show today for the people of Pompeii."

As the guards took hold of Marcus, something exploded deep inside him.

He opened his mouth to scream, to curse Festus and this dark and evil world.

But it was not Marcus's voice that filled the air.

It was the voice of Vesuvius — two shattering explosions.

BOOM!

BOOM!

CHAPTER 13

The ground shook as Marcus had never felt before, as though hundreds of monsters were waking up in their underground caves, pounding the earth in fits of fury.

Panicking, the guards let go of Marcus and Tata. Marcus ran to his father and clung to him, struggling to stay upright as the earth rose and fell like waves on a wild river.

The top of the mountain had blown off, and from the jagged opening gushed an enormous billowing brown cloud. The cloud seemed to stretch into the heavens. Flames shot through the smoke as jagged bolts of lightning ripped at the sky.

People streamed out of the shops. Beggars rose to their feet. Slaves dropped their bundles of wood and water jugs.

For a moment, nobody spoke. Nobody even seemed to be breathing.

All eyes were on the mountain.

But then came the shouts.

"It's the end of the world!"

"Why are the gods punishing us?"

"Everyone must leave Pompeii!" Tata shouted. He started pulling Marcus through the crowd.

But Festus called to his guards. "No! Stop those slaves!" Festus bellowed.

The guards lunged for Marcus and Tata.

But Tata held up his hand. "You must listen!" he boomed. Somehow his voice rose up over the roar of Vesuvius.

To Marcus's shock, the guards did not move. They were just as scared as everyone else.

"If you want to live, you must leave now," Tata warned. He spoke not only to the guards but to the gathering crowd. "Get out of the city, and go as far away from the mountain as you can."

Just then a man stepped out of Festus's chariot. His fine toga swished around his powerful body. In his hand flashed the seal of a senator, one of the most powerful men in Pompeii. But it was not Festus that this man had come out to talk to. It was Tata.

"What you say about the mountain," he demanded. "How do you know this?"

Festus stepped up. "He is just —"

The man silenced Festus with a wave of his hand.

"Speak," he ordered Tata.

Tata did not shrink back from the powerful man. He met his challenging gaze.

"Sir, for years my master was the scientist Linus Selius. My son and I were on the mountain last night. We saw many signs that this disaster

76

was coming. Soon it will be too late to escape with our lives."

The man looked up on the mountain, at the boiling ash cloud that now filled the sky. The mountain's power seemed to be growing. It was now only a matter of time before this blanket of doom fell over the city.

"How much time do we have?"

"A few hours at the most," Tata said. "The worst will come after the mountain runs out of power. I believe all of the gases and ash in the sky will come back down, and explode. A great wave of fire will sweep down over Pompeii."

"Dear gods," the man whispered. A mask seemed to drop from his face, baring his fear. "Festus," he said. "We must warn the magistrates at once! We must order people to leave the city!"

And before Festus could reply, the man had rushed off. With surprising speed, he sprinted across the Forum. He rushed past the guards and disappeared into the government building.

"This is nonsense —" Festus bellowed.

But his words were cut off by a loud *whoosh* from the sky just above them.

Marcus looked up just in time to see a giant flaming fireball closing in on them.

"Look out!" someone screamed.

Tata grabbed Marcus and they dove for cover behind an enormous statue.

And then —

Kaboom!

The flaming boulder hit the street with a deafening explosion.

Small shards of rock showered over Marcus and Tata.

But the explosion had spared them.

They struggled to their feet and made their way back to the street, where a crowd had formed. He heard gasps and wails of shock.

As Tata and Marcus approached, one of Festus's guards turned around.

"The master is dead," he announced.

Marcus peered through the crowd. The boulder had left a shallow crater in the street.

And in the center, lying in a broken heap, was Festus.

Marcus looked away.

He expected to feel happy. Festus was dead!

But it turned out there was no pleasure in seeing anyone's broken body, not even the body of someone as hateful as Festus.

Marcus looked up at the roiling cloud spewing from Vesuvius.

And all he could feel was terror.

CHAPTER 14

It seemed the magistrates had listened to Festus's visitor from Rome. Within minutes, guards were rushing out of the Forum, shouting out warnings.

"Leave the city! Go directly to the gates!" they commanded.

Tata looked at Marcus with relief.

They had done their duty. And now, at last, they could leave Pompeii.

But as they soon discovered, there would be no easy escape.

Marcus and Tata joined the sea of people

streaming down the main street toward the city gates. There were rich men and slaves, parents with babies in their arms and children clutching their robes. Some dragged carts piled high with clothes and dishes and baskets. Others lugged sacks.

As they passed the gladiator barracks, Marcus glanced inside the open gates. There was a man's body lying motionless in the grass, a pillar smashed across his back. With a jolt, Marcus realized it was the lanista. Tata saw him too. But Tata quickly looked away as he tightened his grip on Marcus's hand. Cyclops must be somewhere in this crowd, Marcus realized. But Marcus was no longer afraid of him. Everyone in Pompeii was fighting the same enemy now, the most heartless killer of all: Vesuvius.

Marcus and Tata inched along with the crowd. The sounds from the volcano were getting louder. But most frightening was the darkening sky. An enormous dark cloud had swept down from the mountain. It stretched over the city, turning the day to night. The cloud was black and boiling, and it rumbled with thunder. And then the cloud tore open.

Bits of rock fell from the sky. They were very small and light, almost like bits of ice.

Tata caught some in his hand.

"Hardened ash," Tata said.

Ping, ping, ping, they hit rooftops.

Plop, plop, plop, they splashed into fountains.

They bounced off Marcus's head and shoulders and skittered across the street.

But within minutes, the sprinkling of rocks had turned into a downpour.

The rocks pounded down, hitting the stone streets and rooftops with an earsplitting clatter.

Bam, bam, bam!

The crowd erupted in panic, pushing and elbowing, shouting. Someone shoved Marcus and he almost stumbled. An old woman fell. But the crowd stampeded over her. The rocks seemed to be getting bigger, pounding harder and harder. Dust rose up, making it hard to see.

Marcus clutched Tata's hand. He felt as though they were caught in a stampede of terrified animals.

"Hold on tight!" Tata shouted into Marcus's ear. "I want us out of this crowd!"

They pushed and squeezed their way through, dodging sharp elbows and scratching fingers. Finally, they burst their way out of the crush of screaming people. They hurried into a narrow alley.

"Too dangerous," Tata said breathlessly. "Many people are going to get trampled."

He pulled Marcus into a doorway. They pressed themselves against the wooden door, trying to escape the hail of rocks. But the downpour was even stronger now.

Tata pointed to a small temple just ahead. "We can wait there until it stops."

They pulled their tunics over their heads and waded through the river of stones.

They were just steps from the building when,

Whoosh!

Marcus's heart stopped as he looked up.

It was a huge fireball — bigger than the one that killed Festus.

Kaboom!

The explosion knocked Marcus back. The last thing he saw before he fell was a huge chunk of rock smacking Tata in the head. Marcus hit the ground hard, but within seconds he was back on his feet. He charged over to where Tata lay crumpled on a bed of stones.

Marcus dropped to his knees, grabbing Tata's hand.

"Tata!" he cried.

But Tata just lay there, completely still.

CHAPTER 15

Tata was breathing. Marcus could see that. But then why didn't he open his eyes? Why didn't Tata answer when Marcus called his name? The rock seemed to have knocked him into a deep and terrible sleep, and Marcus could not wake him up.

The storm of rocks continued. Flaming boulders whooshed through the sky, their explosions booming all around. Somehow Marcus managed to drag Tata through the rocks. With a strength he never knew he had, he hoisted Tata up the five stairs that led through the temple's open doorway. He laid Tata on the cold stone floor and collapsed next to him.

Hours passed before Tata's eyes finally fluttered open, and even longer before the fog cleared from his eyes and he could sit up. With each passing minute, it seemed, the mountain's fury grew stronger. The booming and whooshing and thundering and pounding had melded together into a bone-rattling roar. The walls of the temple shook and groaned. They were running out of time, Marcus knew. And then suddenly Tata turned to him.

He took Marcus's hand. "My dear son, it is time for you to go," he said.

"I know," Marcus said. "As soon as you're strong enough we can —"

"No," Tata interrupted. "I'll never make it to the gates. But if you go now you'll still have a chance."

It took a moment for Marcus to understand what Tata was saying: that Marcus should escape by himself.

"No," Marcus said, locking eyes with Tata.

"Please, Marcus. I have thought about this. I have considered every idea. There is no other possibility."

Marcus knew that this was right. But it didn't matter.

"I'm sorry," Marcus said. "But I'm staying here with you."

He looked away so Tata wouldn't see his tears.

And that's when he finally took a good look at the statue that stood right in front of them.

The god with wings on his hat and on his sandals.

Marcus's whole body tingled.

The god was Mercury.

A strange but familiar voice whispered in his mind.

"When hope is lost, follow the hand of Mercury."

The words were so clear, as though the old beggar woman was still right next to him.

Marcus jumped up and went to the statue. He touched the marble, half expecting the statue to turn to flesh and blood, for Mercury to scoop him and Tata into his arms and fly them to the heavens.

"What is it?" Tata said.

He turned to Tata. "That old beggar woman, Tata," Marcus explained. "There was something else she said to me."

He spoke her words slowly to Tata.

Marcus waited for Tata to tell him it was crazy to believe in the ranting words of a stranger.

But Tata didn't shake his head. He stared at the statue intently, studying it.

And Marcus understood that at that moment it didn't matter whether the beggar woman's words were science or magic or madness. Marcus felt the truth of her words in his heart. And so, it seemed, did Tata.

Tata rose to his feet, shaking off his pain and weakness.

"Marcus," he said, his eyes wide with excitement. "Look at the statue's right hand."

Marcus saw it too. It seemed the statue was pointing to something.

But what? The floor was bare.

Unless . . .

Marcus dropped to his knees. He felt around the tile floor until he found a gap between two large tiles.

His heart pounded as he dug his fingers into the gap. There was a groove in the side of one of the tiles. He lifted it up. And he could barely believe what he saw underneath.

There was a trapdoor.

CHAPTER 16

They lifted open the door and peered into the darkness. All they could see was a rickety wooden ladder leading down into the blackness. The smell of sulfur wafted up, stinging Marcus's eyes.

"It must lead to some kind of tunnel," Tata said.

"Where does the tunnel go?" Marcus asked.

"There are tunnels under many Roman cities," Tata said. "Most lead out of the city. People used them to escape in an enemy attack."

But what if this tunnel didn't lead out of the city?

Before he could ask, Tata was climbing down the ladder. He was quickly swallowed by the pitch darkness.

Seconds later his voice echoed up from below.

"Yes, Marcus, it's a tunnel! Come quickly!"

Marcus climbed onto the ladder and fumbled his way down, down, down.

When he reached the bottom, Tata took his arm.

"This way," Tata said, turning him. "Follow closely behind me."

They moved blindly into a narrow passage, crawling on their hands and knees. It was hot as an oven and the passage was so narrow that their shoulders brushed against the rough sides. The stink of sulfur made Marcus gag. Sweat poured into his eyes. His heart hammered. The tunnel seemed endless. And the farther they went, the more terrified Marcus felt.

What if the sulfur killed them? What if the tunnel collapsed?

Marcus tried to fix his thoughts on his heroes, to gather strength from the stories that had always inspired him. He imagined he was Odysseus, braving the wild seas as he returned home from a decade of fighting. He thought of Hercules, fighting the ferocious beasts. But those stories were of no help to him now. His muscles cramped, his arms and legs shook so violently that it was hard to move. A terrifying idea took hold of him: that this tunnel would never end, that he would be forever trapped in this evil darkness. They'd never make it out.

But suddenly his mind flashed to a new story, one that was still being written.

And it was this story that gave Marcus the strength to keep moving.

It was the story of a slave boy who saved his own father by hurling a live cobra through the air, who escaped from killer clouds, leaping flames, and fiery boulders that came hurtling from the sky. He was not favored by the gods or aided by powerful kings. It was the strange words of a mysterious beggar woman that guided him. A tattered mare who carried him. And his father — so wise and good and brave — who showed him the way through the darkness.

It was this heroic boy who kept crawling through the tunnel as tears poured from his stinging eyes, who found the strength to help Tata kick open the door at the end of the tunnel. They clawed through piles of rocks to get to the surface, just outside the city gates of Pompeii. They staggered across a stone-covered field to the olive grove.

The old white mare was waiting for them.

Marcus put his face close to Peg's, looking into her gentle eye. Tata gently brushed away the rocks and ash that covered her coat.

"You waited," Marcus said.

Snort.

Of course she hadn't left them.

Marcus and Tata climbed onto Peg's back.

Without so much as a tap, the mare took off

94

toward Rome. She ran swiftly, her feet barely touching the ground.

They were many miles away when the cloud of ash and gas above Vesuvius collapsed down to earth. The cloud ignited, turning into a flaming whirlwind that blasted down the mountain at speeds faster than any chariot.

Within seconds, the city of Pompeii was burned and buried.

But the horror of Pompeii was now behind Marcus, and all he felt of the mountain's fury was a whisper of heat on his back.

He gripped Tata tightly, and together they looked ahead, for the bright lights of Rome.

BACK IN TIME

I'm always sad to say good-bye to my characters when I finish writing one of my I Survived books. By the time I finally polish up my last draft, my characters seem real to me — dear friends or even family. Marcus and Tata are especially close to my heart, maybe because I had to travel so far back in time to get to know them — almost two thousand years.

I kept reminding myself how very long ago it was that Pompeii was destroyed. It was before the United States was a country, before

Christopher Columbus sailed the seas, before the time of the knights and the great castles of the Middle Ages. Pompeii is in Italy. But two thousand years ago, the country of Italy didn't yet exist. Most of Europe and parts of Africa were all combined in one huge kingdom known as the Roman Empire.

In many ways, life in ancient Roman times was brutal. Slavery was common. Those horrific gladiator shows attracted thousands of delighted fans. Rome's armies were always on the march, conquering new territories and dragging home new slaves. Without medicines and vaccines, most people died young.

But in some ways, life in ancient Pompeii was surprisingly similar to our lives today. Like you and your friends, the kids of Pompeii (those who were not slaves) went to school, learned math, read stories and poems, and played sports. They loved their pet dogs. Just as you obsess over your favorite football or basketball stars, kids of Pompeii were wild about championship gladiators. There were even fast-food restaurants: Pompeii's streets were lined with little stalls that served up soup and stews and bread to people on the go.

I learned all of this during a recent visit to Pompeii. Most of the city has been uncovered and is now an enormous outdoor museum. My husband, David, and I walked through the streets, admired the fountains and statues and mosaics and the graffiti carved into the walls. I even stood in the grassy arena of Pompeii's amphitheater, where thousands of gladiators fought their brutal matches.

It was like traveling back in time, and it was on that trip that I discovered my characters. And of course I met the most frightening "character" of all: the mountain Vesuvius.

There it was, looming over Pompeii just as it did back in AD 79. Vesuvius is now silent and beautiful and green, though it is missing its top, which was blown to pieces in AD 79. But I wasn't fooled. Vesuvius remains one of the most dangerous volcanoes in the world. During my visit, I was always nervously peeking up at that big green mountain, checking for wisps of smoke.

I learned so much while I was writing this book. But as always, there is so much more I want to share with you! So I've thought about the questions that might be on your mind, and tried to come up with clear answers. I hope what you've learned in my book will inspire you to do more research, to take your own trip back in time.

I wish I could go with you.

Nunc valete! (Good-bye for now!)

QUESTIONS AND ANSWERS ABOUT POMPEII AND MOUNT VESUVIUS

How many people died in the eruption of Vesuvius?

There are no records of how many people lived in Pompeii, and how many were killed. But experts estimate that as many as twenty thousand people lived in Pompeii and in its surrounding towns. Of those, between ten thousand and sixteen thousand likely died.

Many people did escape in the first hours after the eruption. Most of those who stayed behind were likely killed by the waves of gases and fire that swept down the mountain. These *pyroclastic surges* traveled at 400 miles per hour, and instantly burned everything in their paths.

What happened to Pompeii after the eruption?

The eruption lasted for three days and buried Pompeii under thirty feet of ash and stone. Word of the disaster reached Rome, and the emperor sent a small team to investigate. But it's unlikely they — or anyone — got too close. For months afterward, the ground must have been very hot. Poisonous gases continued to seep from the earth. There were continuous earth tremors.

In the early years after the eruption, people did try to tunnel into the ruins to find their belongings — or to steal. But as the decades passed, the city was slowly forgotten.

By the year AD 500, the great Roman Empire had crumbled. Cities were invaded by "barbarians"—hordes of fighters from the north and from Asia. These invaders stole whatever they could and destroyed the rest. Most written records of history were lost. Europe was plunged into a terrible time known as the Dark Ages. There was little learning, art, or interest in science and history. People struggled to simply survive during a time of fear and superstition.

How was Pompeii rediscovered?

Many, many centuries passed. The mountain "healed" from the eruption. Grass and trees grew back. People slowly returned to the areas around the mountain. Farmers once again planted olive groves and farms on the slopes. The Dark Ages ended.

By the 1600s, new cities had been born all around Europe and a few bold settlers had headed across the Atlantic Ocean to a strange land called America. People in Europe were interested in learning and discovery again. Many became fascinated by the ancient Roman civilization that had vanished. Around Vesuvius, there were rumors of a beautiful city that once stretched out below the mountain. Every so often a well digger or farmer would discover an intriguing artifact — the arm of a statue, a chunk of a mosaic.

But it wasn't until the year 1764 — nearly 1,700 years after the eruption — when one of the greatest Pompeii discoveries was made: the ruins of a beautiful temple. More dazzling artifacts were soon found.

The early diggers were more interested in snatching whatever treasure they could dig up. But by the 1800s, people realized that Pompeii's artifacts must be preserved and studied. Today, most of Pompeii's treasures are in museums. Excavations of the city have continued steadily ever since, though today at least one quarter of the city is still buried.

Why is Pompeii so important?

There are other places where you can see ruins of buildings from ancient Roman times. The city of Rome is filled with them. But there is no place in the world like Pompeii, which was buried in AD 79 and sealed for centuries, like a time capsule.

The ash and stone preserved more than just the buildings. Archeologists have unearthed thousands of artifacts — skeletons, petrified loaves of bread, statues, toys, furniture, chariots, gladiator helmets, silverware, cooking pots, shoes, earrings, and much, much more.

Most of what we know about life in ancient Rome comes from the discoveries made in Pompeii and a neighboring town called Herculaneum, which was also buried by Vesuvius in AD 79.

Will Vesuvius erupt again?

Yes.

Vesuvius is one of the world's most dangerous volcanoes — and also one of the most closely monitored. It has erupted many times over the past few centuries. None of those eruptions were nearly as powerful as the one that buried Pompeii. But experts have no doubt that another enormous eruption could happen soon.

And this disaster could be devastating. Today, an estimated two million people live in the dangerous "red zone" around Vesuvius. Just fifteen miles north is the crowded city of Naples, where nearly one million people live.

Hopefully, the mountain would give plenty of warning before a major eruption, and people would have time to evacuate. But today, nearly two thousand years after Pompeii was destroyed, we remain powerless against the destructive fury of a major volcanic eruption. Much of this beautiful region of Italy would likely be buried again.

And about the date, AD 79 . . . ?

You might wonder what those letters "AD" stand for.

Today, most of the world uses a calendar that

divides history into two big time periods — the time before Jesus Christ was born and the time after. The time before "year zero" is known as BC, which stands for "before Christ." The time after is known as AD. Many people believe that stands for "after death" — because that would make sense. But AD is actually an abbreviation for the Latin words *Anno Domini*, which mean "in the year of our Lord," indicating the time after Jesus was born. These terms came into use as Christianity spread across many parts of the world. Nowadays, you might see the terms BCE and CE used instead, which mean "Before the Common (or Current) Era" and "in the Common Era."

FOR FURTHER READING
AND LEARNING

My bookshelf is now groaning under the weight of dozens of amazing books about ancient Rome, Pompeii, gladiators, and volcanoes. Here are some of the books I discovered for readers your age.

Ashen Sky: The Letters of Pliny the Younger on the Eruption of Vesuvius, by Pliny, illustrated by Barry Moser
Pliny the Younger was a seventeen-year-old boy when he witnessed the eruption of Mount Vesuvius in AD 79. Years later, he described what he saw in two letters, which are the only eye-witness accounts we have of that eruption.

Bodies in the Ash: Life and Death in Ancient Pompeii, by James M. Deem
Lots of great info about the disaster and the rediscovery of Pompeii.

Eruption! Volcanoes and the Science of Saving Lives, by Elizabeth Rusch, photographs by Tom Uhlman

A thrilling look at some of today's most dangerous volcanoes, and the men and women who study them.

The Buried City of Pompeii, by Shelley Tanaka

An amazing book about Pompeii and the AD 79 eruption, with beautiful illustrations and photographs, and a glimpse into the lives of people who might have lived in the city.

The Secrets of Vesuvius, by Sara C. Bisel

An archeologist shares her experience studying skeletons found in Herculaneum, the town also buried by Vesuvius.